"It has **everything tha...** ... day action, local club rivalry, modern footba... politics, trials, crunching tackles, tricks, misses and goals. It also has everything that today's children need as they grow up. It is jam-packed with positive role models, girls' involvement in Women's Football, respect, mental well-being, good work ethic, education and aspiration." – *Books for Topics*

"Packs a lot of punch in its short and simple to read pages... **It captures the feel of playing and having a passion for football** at an early age very well. More than that it sets out the stall of the new Roy Race, his family background, his friends and enemies, where he lives and his work ethic." – *Comic Scene Magazine*

"**I give it 5,000,000 stars**! I recommend it to 9+ football fans but also non-football fans. I'm not a football fan but I still really enjoyed reading this book. Look out for the graphic novels and the rest of the series. Amazing!" – *The Book Brothers*

"**Football-lovers will love the description of on-pitch action** which is pacy yet satisfyingly detailed. This is a book that I am looking forward to putting on the shelves at school – I know already that it will be a popu... ...ldren

First published 2020 by Rebellion Publishing Ltd,
Riverside House, Osney Mead, Oxford, OX2 0ES, UK

ISBN: 978 1 78108 783 1

10 9 8 7 6 5 4 3 2 1

A CIP catalogue record for this book is available
from the British Library.

Printed in Denmark

Creative Director and CEO: Jason Kingsley
Chief Technical Officer: Chris Kinglsey
Head of Publishing: Ben Smith
Editor: Rob Power   Design: Sam Gretton   Cover image: Lisa Henke

Follow us:

royoftheroversofficial   royoftheroversofficial   royoftherovers

www.royoftherovers.com   info@royoftherovers.com

ALSO IN THIS SERIES

For Rose Hill School, Kent.

A HARD BRIGHT moon illuminated the scene. Two figures moved stealthily, concealed by the black shadow of a long wooden fence, not far from an ageing football stadium. Its hollow, skeletal stands made strange silhouettes against the midnight sky.

It was quiet.

Quiet and late.

The sole witness to the two intruders was a lone vixen, crouching on a nearby canal bank, unused to humans disturbing her midnight world.

Both of the figures looked like young

men, athletic physiques, their heads and faces obscured. One wore a grey beanie hat, the other a black scarf covering his face. You could tell – from their body language – that they were nervous. Maybe even having second thoughts about what they were about to do.

Look closer at the eyes of one and the mouth of the other and you might recognise the two young men. A square jaw. A determined expression. A flop of blonde hair. A pair of piercing blue eyes.

Our two intruders are no delinquents. Nor are they petty thieves or opportunist burglars, making money stealing other people's possessions.

They are professional footballers.

Paco Juan Goytisolo Diaz.

And Roy Daniel Race.

'This cannot be a good idea,' Paco whispered urgently.

'No,' Roy replied in a low almost inaudible voice. 'It probably isn't.'

As Roy spoke, something white and ghostly caught Roy's eye, swooping silently through the row of trees alongside the canal. A barn owl. Roy saw it and smiled faintly. It reminded him of when his dad would take him and his sister on late night nature walks. When he was younger; when his dad was a big strong man and Roy was a boy. But Roy was not a child anymore. And his dad was not such a big strong man.

Times had changed.

'This is your plan?' Paco went on. 'Breaking and entering? I would rather go to Germany on loan than go to prison, Roy Race.'

Roy had questioned what they were about to do a hundred times. Breaking? And entering? Into Mel Park?

It was illegal.

It was immoral.

It was irresponsible.

But did that mean it was the wrong thing to do? Because if this worked, then Roy and Paco's world, Melchester Rovers' world...

even the *whole* world would be a better place.

Roy coughed quietly before he said to Paco what he had said to himself over and over.

'The media reports say that the final contracts for our transfers have gone missing. Those contracts *have* to be in Cleaver's office. Along with, I'll bet, proof of all sorts of dodgy stuff. If we can get in there we can, I dunno, maybe prove to the league that Rovers have done nothing wrong? Maybe we can play again!'

Paco nodded. He knew Roy was right. But that didn't stop him being frightened.

Then – as sudden as the owl-swoop before – they both heard a noise. The crunch of stones under a boot. Roy and Paco stood rigid, peering into the shadows.

Had they given themselves away with

their careless whispering? Were they no longer alone?

A flick of gravel against the wooden fence followed. Roy took a quick intake of breath. There *was* someone there, coming at them from the dark.

Then a voice called out: 'Idiots!'

THE FOOTBALL STADIUM Roy and Paco were about to break into might have looked quiet and calm that night. In fact, it was anything but. Mel Park was in turmoil. The worst turmoil of its one hundred year history. And this was a football club that had seen a lot of ups and downs.

Four months ago the scenes had been of unfettered jubilation. After releasing all of its senior professionals, Melchester Rovers had played an entire League Two season with its youth team – every single player under the age of nineteen. They'd started badly, it was true.

Then something had happened. They gelled. They'd reached for the skies. They fired on all cylinders. Whatever metaphor you chose, Melchester Rovers Football Club – the team who were supposed to be doomed – had been promoted to League One.

Which is when things started to go wrong.

Horribly wrong.

Wanting to cash in on his most valuable assets, Melchester Rovers' owner – Barry 'The Meat' Cleaver – went against the fans' wishes and brought their jubilation crashing to the ground by selling his two best players.

You've already met them. They're standing outside Mel Park, planning to break in.

Paco Diaz, the Spanish winger, was transferred out for £1,000,000.

Roy Race, local striking legend-in-the-making, was sold off by the club he'd loved all his life for £500,000.

And – to make things a thousand times worse – they'd been sold to Melchester Rovers' deadliest, bitterest rivals, Tynecaster United.

After that, what else could go wrong for Melchester Rovers?

Plenty.

The team manager – Kevin 'Mighty' Mouse – suffered a heart attack.

His head coach, Johnny Dexter, resigned in rage at what Barry Cleaver was doing to the club.

And – to add crisis onto crisis onto crisis – the deals to sell Diaz and Race had been dodgy. Dodgier than dodgy. So, the football authorities had been called in to investigate and Melchester Rovers had been found guilty.

The punishment?

They were docked thirty points. So, now

Melchester Rovers needed ten wins before they could even think of trying to climb the table and avoid relegation, bankruptcy and footballing death.

That was why – when the figure emerged from the darkness to accuse Roy Race and Paco Diaz of being idiots – the duo were ready to claim that, even though breaking into Mel Park was wrong, they were doing it for the right reasons.

'IDIOTS!'

Roy and Paco turned, their mouths gaping in shock. They'd been busted. They prepared to run. Then Paco's look of shock turned to a smile.

'Oh,' Diaz said. 'Hello, Ffion. Nice to see you.'

A young woman stood before them, her eyes wide with anger, red hair tied back.

'Shut up, Paco,' Ffion Guthrie snapped, thrusting her hand in his face, glaring at Roy.

'Okay,' Paco said meekly.

17

Ffion grabbed Roy's elbow and led him away from his partner-in-crime.

Roy felt a cocktail of emotions. Shame at being caught. Anger at being caught. Frustration that they would not be able to complete their mission. But, as always, he was pleased to see his girlfriend.

'How did you know I was here?' he asked her. 'I turned my phone off.'

He realised, as soon as he had told her this, that it didn't sound right. He'd turned his phone off: that was true. And he'd done it to keep his girlfriend in the dark.

'I couldn't find you,' Ffion said, lowering her voice, glancing over to see the vixen slink away with something in its jaws, 'so I rang Paco's landlady, who said that you and him were going to Mel Park in balaclavas.'

Roy glanced back at Paco, who was looking quizzically at Mel Park through a small hole in the fence, making out that whatever he had seen in the near distance was far more interesting than Roy and Ffion's argument.

'Brilliant, Paco,' Roy snapped.

'What can I say?' the winger said, not looking round, his attention on what was going on beyond the fence, his eyes squinting. 'Paco is destined to be a superstar footballer and not a criminal mastermind.'

Ffion stared into Roy's eyes, reclaiming his attention.

'How exactly did you plan to get in?' she asked.

Roy smiled at that idea. Had she forgotten that before he was a professional footballer for Melchester Rovers, Roy had been a fan? A fan so obsessed with his team that he had found a way to get into the stadium and sit there alone at night, a solitary worshipper in the church of Melchester Rovers.

'I've been breaking into this place since I was a small boy,' he reminded Ffion. 'It has always been my second home. It's my club.'

A half-smile, half-frown flickered on Ffion's face. 'Not anymore, it's not,' she muttered.

Roy felt as if he'd been slapped. He stepped back and glared at his girlfriend. 'Yes, it is,' he raised his voice. 'Melchester's my club! Melchester will always be my club! I just wanted to help people.' Then his voice broke with emotion, coming out high-pitched like he was an eight-year-old boy again.

Ffion stepped forward, following Roy. She touched his face lightly.

'I'm sorry,' she said. 'I know you didn't want to leave Rovers, but you did. That's all I'm saying.'

'One day I'll be back at this club,' Roy said. 'And I'll help make it great again.'

Ffion nodded. 'I believe it,' she replied.

Roy's voice was fading now, like his anger. 'As you get older,' he said, almost inaudible, 'it all gets out of control, doesn't it?'

Ffion said nothing again. What *could* she say?

She knew that Roy had had a tough time in the last few years. He was a boy of eighteen whose dad was so ill he could neither speak nor walk. Whose mum was worn out from working three jobs to keep the family in their house. Who had left his beloved Melchester Rovers for their bitter rivals, just so that he could make sure that his dad was looked after and his mum wouldn't worry herself to death over money.

'Good intentions,' Ffion said at last. 'But... I think you need someone to keep you out of trouble, Roy Race.'

'Uh... guys?'

Roy and Ffion ignored Paco at first. They were having a moment. And Paco was not part of it.

'GUYS!'

Now the couple looked at their Spanish friend – and at the orange sky behind him on the other side of the fence.

Orange? Roy thought. *Why was it orange?* That wasn't right. The floodlights normally gave off a sharp whitish light. And dawn was hours off. And the sun didn't rise until seven, even half-seven. The light reminded Roy of the kind of glow you get on bonfire night. Warm orange flames.

Then he smelled burning.

'Oh no…' Roy muttered.

Roy could see what was happening, but his brain would not take it in. It was too impossible, too catastrophic.

Paco put his hand on Roy's shoulder

and pointed at what Roy had already seen.
The three friends stared in horror as flames
poured out of the windows above the main
entrance of Mel Park. Orange and red
illuminating the sky above Melchester.

Mel Park was on fire.

ROY GRABBED HIS mobile phone out of his pocket and groaned. It was still switched off. His hands trembled with anxiety as he fumbled to turn it on, the activated screen illuminating his face. But, still, it would take ages for his phone to fire up. They would lose a minute, maybe more.

'Fire service, please,' he heard Ffion say in a calm voice.

Roy turned to see his girlfriend speaking into her mobile phone.

'I'd like to report a fire at the front entrance in the main stand at Mel Park...'

she said. As Ffion spoke, giving all the details the operator needed, the trio stared at the flames as they rushed from a second window, then a third. 'Yes…' Ffion said. 'No… I'm not sure… Okay…. Thank you… We will do that… Thank you.'

Roy could feel the heat of the fire now. And hear what it was doing to Mel Park too. Glass smashing. Wood cracking. Metal groaning. The flames and furnace-hot temperatures were destroying Mel Park.

'Shall we go closer?' Paco asked. 'Maybe we can do something.'

'No.' Ffion shook her head. 'The fire service said to stay away. And there won't be anyone in there at this time of night. It's too late, anyway, Paco. Look.'

'Too late?' Roy mumbled, feeling Ffion's arm around him.

The fire was raging. Mel Park was – room

by room – being destroyed.

Then, out of the corner of his eye, Roy saw a flash against a wall to their left. But not a fire flash. More like a car's lights flashing by. It was near the main entrance.

'A car,' Roy gasped. 'There might be someone in trouble.'

Ffion led the three of them round the corner, through a great curtain of smoke that was hanging low above the car park, and the stench filled their nostrils. They all covered their faces to keep the smoke from their lungs as they saw what was happening.

In front of them there was a car. A slick, black, expensive car. A lone man was holding the back door open, then sliding a cardboard box onto the backseat.

Roy shouted without thinking, 'Are you okay? Can we help?'

The man looked up, shock and malice in

his eyes as they reflected the flames engulfing Mel Park.

Roy recognised him immediately. It was Cleaver. Barry 'The Meat' Cleaver.

The owner of Melchester Rovers didn't stop to exchange pleasantries. He waved his hand with an unpleasant gesture, then

swiftly slammed the back door of his car and dropped himself into the driver's seat.

His headlights came on.

His engine fired.

Then – tyres screaming on the tarmac below – his car was coming at Roy and Ffion and Paco.

Roy heard a scream as he grabbed both of his friends and pushed them around the corner of the wall. It all happened too quickly for them to think or talk about it. Roy acted on instinct as he pressed his body close to the wall and flinched.

Then a crack. A splintering of glass. A rush of air hitting him hard.

And something at his feet.

Roy looked down at a black wing mirror spinning, twisted and smashed and, now, touching his shoe.

Two bricks were missing from the wall

inches from his elbow.

'Arrrgghhh, I hate that man!' Ffion raged.

Roy stepped out into the road to see the taillights of Cleaver's car blinking. The car remained stationary, waiting, like a huge animal breathing heavily before coming back for a second attack.

'He tried to kill us,' Ffion gasped, more subdued now.

The car stayed still for a few seconds. Then sirens. Coming their way. And, as suddenly as it had come at them, the car accelerated away.

'*Did* he try to kill us, Ffion?' Paco asked, his eyes wide and innocent.

Roy had Ffion looked at each other, but didn't reply to Paco. Then – the sirens wailing ever louder – all three of them watched as the main stand at Mel Park seemed to roar in pain and the fire took fatal hold.

EVEN THOUGH SEVERAL days had passed since the night of the fire at Mel Park, Roy could barely operate. His mind was all over the place. There had been so many catastrophic events rolled into that one fateful evening that it had been impossible to think them all through.

The fact that Barry Cleaver had driven his car at Roy, clearly hoping to hit him and his friends, missing by mere inches.

The fact that Roy had been about to break into Mel Park and that Ffion had stopped him committing a crime – and maybe being caught in the fire.

And – worse than all of that put together – the fact that the main stand at Mel Park was a mangled mess of twisted steel and charred wood, putting the future of the football club he loved into jeopardy.

It was too much.

How did you carry on with so many unresolved issues on your mind? How did you live your normal life?

You just did.

That was the answer.

However distracted you were, you couldn't just stop and do nothing, could you?

'RACE!' Roy heard his coach, Ludovico Settembrini, screaming at him. 'Get with it! You're lazy!'

Roy frowned, then heard the voice of the other coach, Hugo. Brazilian international Tynecaster player and friend to Roy. Hugo was doing his training badges, hoping for a career in coaching once his playing days were done. Today, he was helping with the Under-18s Tynecaster development squad.

'Focus on the football,' Hugo smiled, tapping his finger on the side of his head. 'It's just the game now, not outside life. Just your defender to beat, yes?'

Roy was a substitute for the Tynecaster Under-18 development squad on a wet and windy afternoon. For Roy, Settembrini was sort of right. Although Roy was pretty sure that he wasn't lazy, he knew he wasn't really one hundred per cent committed to the game. But Roy preferred Hugo's instructions. It was more helpful to tell a player to focus than to call him lazy. Wasn't it?

Back to the game, trying desperately to focus, Roy studied his opponent. A giant defender, who was marking Roy tightly. The German had pace too. He was so fast, in fact, that since Roy had come on as a substitute in the sixtieth minute, he had been unable to get more than two touches on the ball before he was closed down, blocked or tackled by this one opponent.

Tynecaster Under-18s were playing Deans Park, famous for having the best academy in the country. Players from every continent in the world. Every one of their team was an international, many having made full international debuts.

Hans Castorp – Roy's marker – was a six-foot-four nineteen-year-old from Munich. He was a mountain. A colossus. A giant.

'How do I beat him?' Roy asked Paco during a break in play, as an injured player received treatment. 'I don't have a second before he's on me with one of his telescopic limbs. There's no time, no space.'

'You want the truth?' said Paco, who had

played all of the game's seventy-two minutes so far.

'Of course I do.' Roy frowned at his only friend on the pitch.

'You need to be your old self,' Paco said.

Roy looked at his friend again. The injured player was trying to get to his knees. 'Meaning?'

'You are thinking too much. You are in your head, like Hugo is telling you. Forget your head. Be your body. You understand me? You have time to make one touch of the ball, maybe two, yes?'

'Yes.'

'So, make them count. I play the ball to you. You touch it once. Then you shoot. Comprende?'

'Be more myself?' Roy asked.

'Correct,' Paco said. 'Oh... and stop thinking about that night at Mel Park.'

'But I can't,' Roy complained.

'You must, my friend. You are a footballer. The other things – however hard – are outside the lines of the pitch. You have to leave it there.'

Roy jogged back to his position. Where the German defender was waiting for him with a malicious grin.

'In my pocket,' the mountain said, pointing at his backside.

'Yeah?' Roy said.

'Ja,' Castorp laughed.

The German was right. Roy had never felt so much like someone had him in his pocket. In all his footballing career Hans Castorp was the best defender he'd ever played against. A part of Roy wanted to tell him that after the game. Compliment him. Say: you're the best. I can't beat you.

But another part of Roy knew there was

something else you could do when you came up against your best opposition, your biggest challenges. You had to use the moment to become better yourself. To improve. To find a way to be – like Paco had said – more himself, more the natural footballer he was.

Roy had yet to show his new coaches at Tynecaster the true player they had signed. It was time to change that.

As the Under-18s match wore on, Roy could see that Paco was finding more and more space as the Deans Park right back tired towards the end of the game. Paco was fit. He looked strong. And, remembering how they tore up League Two together the season before, Roy decided to work down the centre of the pitch, then run in sharp sudden angles, right or left just before arriving in the penalty area. He hoped the combination of speed and unpredictability would fox his German shadow.

Roy knew from experience that Paco

would wait to play the ball in just as Roy made his move, hopefully reading Roy's run. The German had no idea what Roy was going to do. But Paco would: they had played over a season together at Melchester and Johnny Dexter always said they had a telepathic relationship.

Roy missed Johnny Dexter, their old coach. There was a man who could say the right thing at the right time to get the best out of Roy on the pitch – and off it.

Most of the times Roy tried his planned move, Hans Castorp got to the ball first. But you had to work, work, work to create chances and, over the twenty minutes Roy and Paco had together, there were three times where, using all his pace and guile, Roy beat the German to it.

The first time, Roy controlled the ball and tried to turn the defender, who had already put himself between Roy and the goal. But Hans Castorp put in a perfect tackle.

Roy smiled back as the defender grinned at him.

'Great tackle,' Roy said.

The German's eyes sparkled as he glared at Roy.

And Roy heard Hugo on the touchline. 'That's it, Roy Race. Keep that up. Keep making chances to make chances, yes?'

Roy nodded.

The second time he had control of the ball, Roy dummied to let it run through his legs, hoping to fool the defender into missing it, thus leaving him free goal side with the ball – with Paco running in the channel alongside him.

That was the plan.

But the plan failed. The defender read the move and passed it up field, leaving Roy bearing down on goal. Without the ball.

Roy jogged back into position, and the German kept eye contact with him.

'Well read, mate,' Roy said.

The German laughed. 'I will read you like a book all day long,' he told Roy.

The third time Roy ran a deeper angle, closer to the penalty area, meaning Paco's

chip hit the pitch, then bounced higher than before to Roy at waist level, back to goal, Castorp behind him.

Roy twisted, making a quick space between himself and the ball, then he smacked it first time.

Left foot. Hard and low. With as much power as he could muster.

Roy fell onto his backside after the ball had gone. Not because he needed to, but he wanted to see what he knew he would see. The ball arrowing into the top left corner of the net, the keeper not imagining a shot from that position.

Goal.

The defender had forced him to try something new. To be better. To use his instinct. And Roy had done it.

A hand came down to lift Roy back onto his feet.

It was Hans Castorp.

'Magic,' the mountain said.

Roy and the German shook hands. Then Roy jogged back to the halfway line nodding thanks to Paco on the wing and noticing Hugo and the head coach, Settembrini, both applauding.

Behind them he saw another figure. Large, huge-shouldered, hoodie up, his face hidden. But Roy didn't really register the man, now he was one hundred per cent focussed on the game. He seemed so familiar that, at the time, Roy didn't question who he was.

And, for a few seconds, as Paco had suggested, Roy realised he had forgotten about Cleaver and Mel Park and the fire and all the other things crowding his mind. Now he was thinking about football, about playing well enough in the Under-18s to get a spot on the bench in the Tynecaster first team.

That was the plan. After the final whistle. Talk to the coach. Push himself into the frame. Be more himself.

AFTER THE GAME, Roy looked for the large man in the hoodie. He knew who he thought the man was, now he had time to think about it.

Johnny Dexter, his coach from Melchester.

But there was no giant hoodied man looking on now. Roy frowned and decided he had been seeing things. Johnny Dexter? Here? At Tynecaster United?

That was doubtful. The man hated the place.

Puzzled, Roy decided to hang back to speak to the Under-18s coach, Ludovico Settembrini. He wanted to ask him if he could start for the Under-18s, even tell him he was keen to be on the first XI bench for the first time. Just to put the idea out there.

Now that the game was over and the players were straggling back to the dressing rooms, the pitch where Roy had played for the Under-18s seemed just like any other pitch, except for tall wire fences up one side, a raised platform with cameras for monitoring training, and the fact that the pitch was as perfect a field of grass could be for fast-passing football.

Hugo and Paco Diaz had already headed off to the dressing rooms.

'Mr Settembrini?' Roy asked as the Italian ghosted past him in the corridor outside the dressing room.

The Italian sighed audibly and stopped.

'Mr Race?' Settembrini threw his voice with a flourish, as if they were a couple having a conversation on a stage. 'You want to tell me you need more? You want to be more than a substitute for the Under-18s? You want to play for the first team?'

Roy heard a few of his Tynecaster teammates laughing at what his coach had said to him. Then he saw that some of them were lingering, waiting to hear what Settembrini would say.

'Er…' Roy stuttered. 'Yes, that's what I wanted to say.'

'Your goal, Race, was very good. Your timing. Your strength. But look around you. Here we have boys from academies in Milan and Rio and Madrid. They are all very good. They are strong. They have good timing. And they have learned this playing against Juve, Barca and more. You? You have never left Melchester, no?'

Roy wanted to say he'd played in a

tournament in the Arctic Circle, but he stopped himself before he made a fool of himself. His teammates looked keen to see that happen. Paco was standing there too, a look of concern on his face.

'I have something for you though, Race,' Settembrini said, looking inspired.

'Really?' Roy said.

'An important job. For you to represent the club. Where I know you will be the best footballer on the pitch.'

'Great,' Roy said, oblivious to the smirks on the faces of his teammates and the car crash expression of Paco Diaz. 'Tell me where and when?'

Roy was excited. Maybe this was his chance to show that he was exceptional. Maybe that goal he had scored had finally made Settembrini see him for the footballer he could be?

THE MOVE TO Tynecaster had been very difficult for Roy in a lot of ways. He hated being away from Melchester Rovers. He hated being powerless to do anything to help his old club, too. He hated being in the Under-18s: having developed a taste for first team action at Mel Park. Although he knew that every player had to earn his or her place in any team.

But there was one way the move had made life better.

The money.

Roy had gone from earning £800 a week to £8,000 a week. For Roy, money was secondary to football, but for his family it was everything. That – after all – was why he had made the move from Rovers to United.

And today was a day that that money made a huge difference. Big bucks were meant to change lives – and they did.

Especially his dad's life.

Especially today.

Because today was the day that his dad's chairlift was fitted. Once the two women fitting the chairlift had finished, the Race household had a rail running up the wall-side of the narrow staircase. At the foot of the stairs there was a metal platform that folded out when his dad was ready to go upstairs. It nearly touched the front door, their wallpapered hallway was so tight. But it worked. And that was what mattered. His dad could secure himself in, then go up to his bedroom and the bathroom when he chose to.

It was time for a test drive.

Dad pressed the button to move his chair lift with his left hand and slowly began to ascend the stairs, the machine giving off a grinding, whirring sound. Mum, Rocky and Roy smiled as Dad travelled up the chairlift for the first time.

But the smiles were tense smiles. Because everything was so weird. A machine taking dad up the staircase that he used to be able to bound up in five strides, Roy on his shoulders screaming with delight.

That was why it was weird.

They couldn't see if Dad was smiling as he made his first ascent. His face was turned away, so they had no idea how Dad was feeling.

'When was the last time you were upstairs?' Mum said, trying to break the tension.

Dad didn't answer. He rarely managed to get a word out. Once a week if they were lucky.

'A year?' Rocky suggested. 'More. A year and a half.'

Mum, Rocky and Roy stood in silence pondering that fact. Eighteen months for

Dad: stuck with only the front room, kitchen and a temporary loo and shower in the back room.

As Dad reached the top of the stairs, Mum started clapping. She was smiling. She didn't look quite as tired as she used to, Roy thought. The children joined in with the clapping. At the top, Dad turned round and they saw his face for the first time. He was grinning.

This was why Roy liked the Tynecaster money. He didn't want it for himself. In fact, Roy gave his mum all his money, except £100 a week that he kept for magazines, coffees, games, and food while he was on the move.

Mum had paid for this chairlift with it. She'd hired a carer to come in and help five days a week. She and Rocky had gone clothes shopping and had both had their hair done. They were talking about booking a holiday in the summer. Things were changing. Changing for the better.

Mum mouthed a *Thank you* to Roy, before she headed upstairs to help Dad. Rocky went up to her room.

Roy went into the kitchen alone. He grabbed a glass of water, and sat at the table and sighed. Things were better at home because of the Tynecaster money. There was no doubting that. And he was quite sure that it was worth it.

It used to be that his problems were at home and football was an escape from it: but now it was the other way round. Home was improving. Football was the source of his troubles.

GATESFIELD VERSUS MELCHESTER Rovers on a bleak mid-week night. An away game. Dark skies illuminated by fifty-year-old floodlights that seemed to burn into the back of Roy's retinas.

But here he was. Back with the team he loved, even if he was sat in the stand. They were winning 1-0. Roy tracked the action carefully as Vic Guthrie muscled his way over the halfway line, checked, then fired a daisy-cutter wide to Zhang Wei on the right wing.

Another attack.

Before the game Ffion had asked Roy to go and sit on his own as she and Rocky talked to a group of Melchester fans. They called themselves Militant Melchester. They were discussing a plan to get rid of Barry Cleaver, remove him from the club. Roy knew Ffion was part of the plotting, a secret group of Rovers fans who wanted to stop the rot at

the club. And – however much it hurt to see her chatting and laughing with Melchester fans – he understood why she didn't want him there.

He was Tynecaster. Full stop.

They wouldn't want him there.

Once the game kicked off, Roy did his best to focus on the game, even though Ffion and Rocky, next to him, were talking about another game: one they were playing in three days for their own team, Sowerby FC. It was a big one, too. A cup game that could see them raise their profile as one of the area's top women's teams.

'I can't cope with this,' Roy said, putting his hands flat to the sides of his head like a horse's blinkers. And it was true. Roy had always found it impossible to talk about one game while watching another. He couldn't keep it all in his head.

Roy felt his legs twitch as his instincts told him to move upfield. He moved his legs to the left and stretched his calves. This was impossible. He felt like he was chained to the stands.

Restless.

Then a hand on his knee. Ffion's hand.

'Stop jiggling your legs and jerking around in your seat,' she said calmly. 'You'll draw attention to yourself. Don't forget you're Roy Race, Melchester Rovers' public enemy number one at the moment.'

Roy shrugged. He couldn't help himself. This always happened when he watched football: it was as if his body thought he was down there on the turf. The stadium was half full, the floodlights now glaring off the yellow plastic seats of the home team's stands. The noise of the players' shouting echoed off the empty stands too, when the away fans – two thousand from Melchester – paused to take a break from singing their songs.

It was a rundown stadium at a club that had no money now, and hadn't had any money for decades. But at least, Roy reflected, their stadium was intact.

The morning after the fire he had jogged down to Mel Park on his way to training with Tynecaster United and had seen the smoking mess of twisted metal and charred wood. Where the main stand at Mel Park once had been there was now a gap. Fire engines still dousing the embers with gallons of water.

Roy's eyes turned back to the pitch, and he tracked Wei as he took the ball down the by-line and flicked an early looping cross over to the far post. Patrick Nolan and Vernon Elliott were in the area. Roy too: in his imagination. He jumped up from his seat.

'Idiot!' Rocky said, slapping him on the

back of his hoodie. 'Sit. Didn't you hear Ffion?'

Roy sat, disappointed to see the ball sail over both his former teammates' heads. This was unbearable. He had imagined that, if he showed up to watch Melchester away with a hoodie up, he'd be able to support his team without drawing attention to himself.

He was wrong.

'Roy?' Rocky snapped again, using the high-pitched posh voice of their old head teacher from primary school, the voice she used to try to make Roy stop fidgeting. 'If you can't sit still, then you need to go to the back of the hall.'

His sister was laughing now. Ffion too.

'Fine,' Roy said, climbing over a seat and smiling at the two girls. 'You two were doing my head in anyway. You're spending more time talking about your match next week than this one. I can't concentrate.'

Head down, hoodie up, Roy walked to the back of the half-empty stand, nobody within fifty metres of him, just row after row of upturned plastic seats. Rocky and Ffion could talk about their big game coming up to their hearts' content. And it would be easier to enjoy the game stood up, anyway. Then he could move onto the ball or stretch to reach it without being restricted by a seat.

He leaned his back against a wall. At the top of the wall was one of the executive boxes at Gatesfield, where business people sat behind glass doors and drank and ate as the game went on. They could watch the game from a balcony outside the glass doors, but that sort of fan rarely did. The drink and food meant more to those fans than the football, Roy had always thought.

Except today there *was* someone at the balcony.

The man on the balcony was leaning his elbows on the top of Roy's wall. He was smoking a cigar and talking into his phone in a quiet voice. Roy recognised the aroma of the cigar. Who else would smoke inside a building nowadays? Only an arrogant self-obsessed idiot. Only someone who had no respect for every other person on the planet.

Roy backed up and pressed his body against the wall. This was the last man in the world he needed to see. The last person in the world he wanted to see *him* after the events at Mel Park.

This man with the cigar was Barry 'The Meat' Cleaver.

ROY CHECKED HIS hoodie was concealing his face, and stayed dead quiet.

He didn't like seeing the Melchester Rovers owner at the best of times, but it was only a few days since the man had tried to run him down. And Roy was still not convinced Cleaver hadn't recognised him back on the night of the fire.

'I'm away this weekend,' Cleaver said to his interlocutor. 'No... no... she's away too. Going to somewhere in Spain with her girlfriends. Tuscany or somewhere. I dunno. And I don't care. Ha ha. No... I'm going to play golf in Portugal. Seventeenth to the twentieth. Without her, thank the lord.'

Roy rolled his eyes. That was nice.

'No, the dogs won't be in,' Cleaver went on. 'She's putting them in kennels.'

Roy's mind started working, as he watched the game, Melchester getting more and more time on the ball in their opponent's half, as

the home team backed off deeper and deeper. Cleaver was going away all weekend. So was his wife. The man didn't have children. And his dogs were going to be in kennels.

'A taxi's coming for me at ten, Friday morning,' Cleaver finished. 'Back home Monday late. Yeah… cheers.'

After another couple of minutes, the smell of sweat and cigar smoke faded and Roy heard a sliding door lock.

Cleaver had gone. He hadn't noticed Roy was there, hadn't realised Roy had overheard his plans. Roy glanced at his phone to check the dates the Melchester owner had mentioned. Friday to Monday. Roy had an idea. An idea that he hoped would save Melchester Rovers. Another chance to put things right.

He opened his mouth to speak and looked down at Ffion to see his girlfriend and sister jumping up and down in their seats. Then the noise from the away end hit him. A roar of two thousand Melchester voices.

GOAL!

Roy gazed at the pitch to see his old friend, Lofty Peak, wheeling away from the Gatesfield goal, his hands in the air. And now, as the cheers of the red and yellow faithful faded, Roy could hear boos, from the home fans, echoing through the stadium and into the night.

The scoreboard read:

Gatesfield 0 – 2 Melchester Rovers
85 minutes

The game was won. Roy punched the air and roared: 'Yeaaaaahhhhhhssss.' Then held his breath in case Cleaver was there again.

And he was. Back out there pacing around

the balcony outside the executive box. But he'd still not seen Roy. He was too busy swearing into his phone.

'What's wrong?' Cleaver shouted down the phone. 'I'll tell you what's wrong. Melchester bloody Rovers have won. Again. And the more they win the less likely it is for me to be able to sell the ground and build two hundred houses on it.'

Roy shook his head.

'Why?' Cleaver went on. 'Because the council and the fans, especially that Militant Melchester mob, will have more power, more fuel for their fire. I need them miserable and without hope. I need them as burned out and collapsed as that stadium they so adore, so that they give up. My God, I hate this club and everyone who's part of it. I almost feel like destroying it just to get back at that lot – even if I do lose a load of money.'

'So... TONIGHT... I overheard something at the match,' Roy said to Ffion and his sister.

They'd left the stadium and were driving away into the rainy darkness of a Gatesfield night for a two-hour journey home, Rocky in the front with Ffion.

Roy had been desperate to sit next to Ffion in the front. He'd been fine with Rocky sitting up front with Ffion on the way, because his sister had promised he could sit there on the way home. Then she'd broken her promise and lunged for the front seat, Roy trying to drag her out of the car, both of them laughing hysterically, until Roy saw two burly Gatesfield fans watching them and he wondered if he and his sister didn't look like siblings fighting over a front seat, and gave up before one of the men came to Rocky's defence.

Roy leaned forward in between the two front seats, now he had their attention.

'What?' Rocky laughed. 'Both sets of fans singing that song about Roy Race being a...'

'Cleaver,' Roy interrupted.

'Cleaver?' Ffion asked, slowing down to glance over her shoulder at Roy.

'He's lying,' Rocky said. 'He just wants your attention, Ffion.'

Roy shrugged. 'Fine. Forget it. I'll just...'

'Tell us, Roy,' Ffion said. 'Anything to do with Cleaver is to do with me.'

So Roy told them. Barry Cleaver would be playing golf in Portugal this weekend. His wife would be sunning herself with her best friends abroad. And Cleaver's pack of three vicious guard dogs would be in the kennels.

The house would be empty.

'So?' Ffion sounded excited. 'What are you suggesting we do about it?'

'I dunno,' Roy said, desperate to be part of whatever Ffion was planning against Cleaver with the other Melchester fans. 'I mean… maybe we could go in… you and me, Ffion?'

'And me,' Rocky said.

They drove in silence, the windscreen wipers scraping an uneasy rhythm. Roy thought about Melchester Rovers, how they had lost thirty points and were under investigation by the football authorities. And how their owner wanted to sell them and turn the stadium into a housing estate. What was left of the stadium after the catastrophic fire. How... in effect... they were doomed.

He sighed.

'So we go in?' Ffion broke the silence. 'We break into his house? Really?'

'Yeah?' Roy said. He knew she was interested. He could tell by her tone of voice. Maybe she was impressed with him: that he'd had such an idea.

'And me,' Rocky said again.

'Fire,' Ffion mused. 'Thirty points. Your dodgy contract. Cleaver. He's the common link. Am I right? The only way the club can be saved is if a hero comes along and breaks a small rule. And that hero is...'

'Me,' Roy finished her sentence.

'Roy always ends up the hero,' Rocky grumbled. 'I should be the one who does it this time.'

Roy ignored his sister's remark. 'We need evidence,' he insisted, 'to prove what

Cleaver has done. And that means we need the contents of the box that he took from the stadium and put in his car. Because I bet they're the files that could help us sort this out. If we don't get it, Melchester Rovers are dead. Someone has to be the hero.'

'Me,' Rocky said again.

'No way,' Roy said.

'We'll see...' Rocky said. Then – after a pause – added: 'We should tell Johnny Dexter?'

'What?' Ffion and Roy said together.

'Tell him. He needs something. He's miserable. Can't you see how sad he is when he comes to train Sowerby? He needs something to give him meaning. His one love in life is Melchester Rovers. He'd break every law in the world to save them, surely?'

'He might warn us off,' Ffion said cautiously.

Roy sat back in his seat.

This was interesting.

Could he and Ffion get hold of the papers in Cleaver's house? Could he do something to make him feel less wrong about leaving Mel Park?

Things were looking up.

TWO NIGHTS LATER Roy had his chance to talk to Johnny Dexter.

They were standing together watching Sowerby FC versus Northowram FC in the quarter final of the Northern Women's Cup at the Melchester Municipal Sports Centre, where Ffion and Rocky's team played all their home games.

Dexter had been appointed head coach by Ffion. Ffion said that she needed him, so that she could concentrate on her game and on captaining the side. But Roy knew there was more to it than that.

Ffion cared about Johnny.

Johnny needed something to take his mind off the car crash that was Melchester Rovers. And this job was perfect for him.

'It's win-win,' she'd told Roy when he'd asked her why she needed Dexter.

'What about me?' Roy had asked. 'Why am I here?'

'Eye candy for the girls,' Ffion said, before bursting into peals of laughter.

Roy never got to the bottom of why Ffion wanted him at their games week on week, but he knew why he was there today. To talk to Coach about the box of papers they'd seen Cleaver take from Mel Park on the night of the fire. If Roy could get Johnny's support and his advice, they might be able to find a way of saving the club that he lived for. It was just up to Roy to find the right moment and the right way of raising it with him. Where better than on the touchline, watching the game, chatting over ninety minutes?

It would also give him a chance to confront Johnny about whether he'd been watching Roy play for the Tynecaster Under-18s. The big guy in the hoodie. Could it have been him?

It was a great opportunity. But Roy still

felt anxious. Was Johnny Dexter the right person to talk to? He'd already told him he had something he wanted to talk to Johnny about. And his former coach had said he could talk to him about anything he wanted, any time.

But Roy said nothing for the first ten minutes as the two teams tested each other out. For Roy they seemed evenly matched. Pace up front. Solid defences, both playing deep to deal with the forwards. The game was too tense for them to talk about Melchester as well. Roy imagined Johnny was the same as him: one game at a time. Focus on what was in front of you.

The first move saw Northowram take a quick throw in, catching Sowerby off guard. The visiting midfielder was about to spray the ball wide as her teammates poured forward, but she took too long and Rocky was onto her, forcing her to turn and shield the ball. Then, the midfielder showed too much of the ball, and Rocky lunged in, clipping it to safety, taking the player with her.

There was a cry of complaint from the Northowram side of the pitch. Four or five of their support team claimed a foul. But the referee waved play on.

'Fair tackle,' she called out.

Roy caught his sister's smile as she got back to her feet. That look she had – of grim pleasure – tackling someone harder than she maybe needed. No-one knew the dark side of Rocky Race like Roy did. He was quite pleased she'd found an outlet for it other than winding him up.

Johnny Dexter nodded to Roy. 'Your lass,' he said. 'Nothing like you, is she? Good... I mean... she's good. But you two are like chalk and cheese. You... you're all class and skill. But your sister,' Dexter grinned, 'she's a bit more like I was on the pitch…'

'Not like me playing for Tynecaster, then?' Roy asked.

Johnny's face flickered with a smile, then he hid it with a frown.

'Don't know what you mean,' he said, gruffly.

'No?'

'No.'

'So I didn't see you watching Tynecaster Under-18s. Watching me and Paco.'

Johnny shook his head.

'In their reserve stadium,' Roy said.

'Never been to Tynecaster. Never will.'

Roy could see Johnny was laughing now, his face turned away, looking up and down the touchline at the crowd that had built up, ready to change the subject. There were over a hundred people watching on the Sowerby side of the pitch. Roy saw Coach studying them too, his hands deep in his pockets, shoulders sloping.

'Who are all these people?' Johnny Dexter asked.

'Fans?' Roy suggested. He'd decided to leave the Tynecaster question for now.

'Like proper fans?' Coach asked. 'The team has a following?'

'The women's game is growing,' Roy said. 'If we win this we're in the semis of a cup. A proper cup.'

'Good then,' Coach rubbed his hands together. 'You know, I could get into this. A bit more fun than life under Barry Cleaver.'

Roy reflected on Johnny Dexter. What was it about him? Was it his voice? Or his sloping shoulders? The way he asked questions now, rather than barking out orders. He certainly wasn't the same man who had begun coaching Roy at Melchester Rovers exactly a year before.

Was he… happy?

But – as the game went on – Roy noticed Coach become more animated.

At one point in the game, Ffion switched sides of the pitch. Roy knew why. She wanted to get close to Johnny, to talk tactics and influence the game, as it had stagnated into defensive back passing. Ffion tracked the opposition winger and – when the winger tried to play the ball past her – Ffion wellied it hard over the fence, so that one of the subs had to run and get it.

'Too cautious!' Coach told Ffion. 'You have to push more men… sorry, women… forward when you bring the ball out. Take risks or you might as well pack it in.'

Ffion put her thumb up, then put her hands on Roy's shoulders, making out she was stretching his calves. But she wasn't.

Ffion looked hard into Roy's eyes. 'We're doing this, right?'

'What?'

'The heist.'

'Cleaver's?'

'Yeah.'

'Sure,' Roy nodded.

'You and me. Keep it between us, yeah?'

'Yeah,' Roy agreed, ducking as he sensed the ball flying at him from behind. It was. Ffion caught it, two hands to her chest, smiling. Then she was off. Roy watched Ffion back on the pitch, organising her team. She was shouting at her players, telling them to push on, putting an arm round others, speaking to them calmly.

Roy sensed the game was going to change. It needed a goal. And a goal was coming.

THE GOAL CAME a few minutes after Johnny's intervention.

Ffion on the ball, moving forward steadily as the Northowram midfield backed off. Ffion touched it to Rocky, then ran forward. Rocky shouldered off a tackle then ran with the ball, through the centre of midfield.

Roy squinted and studied how his sister managed to move through three or four defending players, the ball at her feet, but so smoothly that no-one could tackle her. It seemed effortless. But Roy knew that the easier it looked the better the player was.

His sister – he realised – was becoming an essential player in the team. She was good. Really good.

Looking to her left, Rocky played the ball to her right, fooling everyone.

Hard.

Fast.

Unexpected.

And there was Ffion. In on goal. One touch to control it, then a shot pinging in off the post. The keeper just stood there, too surprised to even try to save it.

GOAL!

Sowerby were winning 1-0.

From nowhere.

Roy felt Johnny's hand on his shoulder. 'She's a good one, your sister,' Coach remarked, punching the air. 'That pass. My God. You've taught her well.'

'I taught her nothing,' Roy said.

'I know. I can see it clearly.' Johnny Dexter laughed and Roy decided this was the moment to ask his advice about the box of paperwork in Barry Cleaver's house.

'You know... I could get into this,' Johnny interrupted Roy's thoughts, straightening his back and stretching his arms, repeating what he'd said earlier. 'Just what I need after all the… well, you know… after all the trouble at Rovers. It hit me hard, you know, Roy. But this? Helping Ffion and the girls out. I like it. There's nothing to worry about but good, honest football. No Cleaver. That's what I like about it. No…' Coach's voice turned into a growl, '… nothing to do with that man.'

'Right,' Roy said. 'Yeah…'

The smile on Roy's face faded when he understood that he wasn't going to tell Johnny Dexter about Barry Cleaver's house after all. How could he? The man had been through enough upset and risk and trauma. And now he looked a little happier.

'So,' Coach said. 'What was it you wanted to tell me?'

'Nothing,' Roy said, wishing he'd not mentioned it to Coach now.

'Nothing? It didn't sound like it earlier.'

'I changed my mind.'

Coach shrugged and turned his attention back to the game, Rocky tackling one player hard, going to ground, then leaping again to trap the ball and shield it from a Northowram player.

'Good,' Johnny shouted. 'Keep it up, Rocky Race.'

Roy frowned.

Johnny praising his sister.

That didn't feel one hundred per cent great.

He felt a sharp pang of envy towards his sister. He wanted that for himself. Wanted Coach's approval and, even, affection. He missed it all: Coach and Mouse and Melchester Rovers, that world and that life; everything Barry Cleaver was destroying.

Roy breathed in. He would get that back. One day.

But Johnny Dexter was not the right man to go to for advice: Roy was quite sure about that. Johnny was happy. He was even smiling. He had a new lease of life. Why spoil things for him? There was no way he was going to be Roy's confidant.

So who – if anybody – was?

ROY HAD THE perfect chance to tell an adult what he was planning to do. His mum's birthday. She'd understand, surely? She was a massive Melchester Rovers fan, just like the rest of the Race family.

Roy had already planned to take her out for afternoon tea. They'd had it in the diary for weeks. He had even booked a table.

Afternoon tea in a posh hotel on the edge of town. Cups of tea. Sandwiches with the crusts cut off. Small cakes and scones. In a room with a large chandelier in the centre of the ceiling and purple flowery wallpaper.

Each table had a small bunch of white flowers that smelled, to Roy, quite appealing. He had no idea what sort of flowers they were.

There were three waitresses and one waiter, all dressed in white shirts and black trousers and waistcoats. Roy caught the waiter and one of the waitresses pointing at him and whispering. It might be because he was a footballer. It probably was. He knew that. Though it might not be. Maybe he had some cake in his hair, or something?

Afternoon tea in a posh hotel was Roy's mum's idea of heaven, but not Roy's. However, from the huge grin on his mum's face as Roy poured her tea from the china teapot, it was enough for him that *she* was in heaven.

Roy had been talking about playing for Tynecaster. How it was hard.

'You just need to be yourself,' Mum said.

'Look, I hope you don't mind me saying, but, at Mel Park, you were carefree. Now you play like you're dragging a weight around with you. I've not seen much Roy of the Rovers recently: more Roy of Tynecaster United.'

'It doesn't sound as good, does it?' Roy grinned.

Mum took a sip of tea and sighed.

'No, I'm afraid not, my love, but I can tell you that this is lovely,' she enthused. 'Out for afternoon tea with my handsome footballer son. Just the two of us on my birthday. Rocky is at school. I've got you away from Ffion for once. Your dad is with his new carer. I just…'

Roy watched his mum falter, then dab her napkin into the corner of her eye. Things were good. Well, not good. But they were better. With the chairlift and the other new equipment they had, as well as carers to help during the day, Dad seemed a lot better. He was still immobile and barely said a word, but his mood was positive, he was eating well, he even looked a bit more like his old self.

And, if Dad felt better, then Mum did too.

'...want to say... this is lovely...' she added.

Roy was about to speak when his mum put her hand on his across the table.

'Do you know?' Mum said. 'For the... for the first time in a long time... I feel happy.'

Roy felt himself choke a little on his scone. He never thought he'd hear his mum say those words again: *I feel happy*.

Roy picked up another scone and stuffed it into his mouth. Now he felt happy. Too happy. The sort of happy that made him feel a little bit sad, somehow. Emotional, maybe.

'No cream?' Mum asked, looking at Roy as he munched through his scone.

Roy shook his head. 'Tynecaster orders,' he said, with his mouth full.

His mum eyed him like she used to when he was five or six. The don't-speak-with-your-mouth-full look.

Roy chewed with his mouth shut, looking at his plate.

'Thank you for this, Roy,' Mum filled the silence. 'I can't thank you enough for what you've done. Dad, yes. But me too. Giving up all those jobs. Life is a lot easier for us. That's why I'm saying I am happy. You've done this for us.'

Roy couldn't speak. If he did, he'd cry. He had to keep a lid on it.

He was pleased to see his mum pull some booklets out of her bag.

'Look,' she beamed.

Roy looked. He recognised what the booklets were. College prospectuses.

'I was thinking of asking your dad and you and Rocky if you'd mind if I...'

'Mum. Just do it. You have to. You've given us so much over the years and never had a chance to... never thought about yourself...'

And now Roy was crying. He looked down at his scone and tried not to, but it came. He had too many thoughts in his head about his dad, his mum, his football. It was overwhelming.

Roy felt his mum's hand on his shoulder.

'You're a good lad,' she said.

Roy shook his head. 'Stop,' he said. 'I can't...'

Mum stopped talking. And, as Roy tried to calm himself down, breathing heavily, he knew there was no way he was going to tell his mum about breaking in to Barry Cleaver's house at the weekend.

She was happy.

She'd only worry and be unhappy again. Roy wanted her to dream about going to college, then to go to college, then to enjoy it and learn and do what she wanted to do for herself in the world. He would not tell Mum.

So, who was left to tell?

Dad?

Of course.

Roy would tell his dad. His dad would listen. His dad would understand.

'YOU'RE SUBSTITUTE TONIGHT,' Settembrini told Roy after a gentle morning training session at the Tynecaster training complex.

'What game?' Roy asked, puzzled.

There was only one game scheduled for tonight and that was Tynecaster United first team versus Lobo Antunes FC of Portugal in the Champions' League. No Under-18s. No development squad. No behind-closed-doors friendlies.

'*That* game,' Settembrini grinned. 'You say you want to prove you are a player. So, you prove it, maybe?'

Roy couldn't believe it: he might be about to make his Champions League debut!

So, when he walked into the dressing room that evening, he attempted to wear an expression that looked confident, even cocky. You had to pretend you were something you were not at Tynecaster, he had discovered. If everyone else wore a disinterested expression all the time, he figured he ought to do the same to fit in.

The French international – Guy de Flaubert, holder of a World Cup winners' medal – was the only person in the dressing room, busy spraying his leg with something in an aerosol can and swearing under his breath.

He looked up as Roy entered.

'Look at your face, boy!' he said. 'You maybe need to lavatory? Yes? Nervous maybe? I am not surprised if you are nervous. But this match… it does not matter. We have already topped our group. Lobo Antunes FC? They are eliminated. This is a dead match. It means nothing. *This* is why you play.'

Roy said thank you to Guy de Flaubert. Though he wasn't sure what he was saying thank you for.

RUNNING OUT ON the pitch an hour later, Roy was still nervous. His disinterested grin had become a tight-lipped frown. He was too nervous and he hated it. There was nothing worse than nerves when it came to stopping him do his best. A few nerves were good, even useful. But nerves that made you over-think and burn your energy off were not good.

But now he was on the pitch, Roy noticed something. Something strange about the atmosphere in the stadium.

The crowd was made up of children.

Roy looked around him and into the stands. All he saw was row after row of children.

'Ten thousand of them,' his fellow substitute, Dan Cornwell, told him. 'There were ten thousand tickets unsold for the game. So... the manager gave them all away to school children. Crazy, eh?'

Roy nodded. 'Yeah...' he said. 'Crazy...'

But something told Roy that this was not crazy. Playing in front of ten thousand children sounded good. They'd be excited and positive. They wouldn't be disappointed to see Roy and all the other second-string players play. If he put on a show, did well, they'd respond.

Wouldn't they?

Roy settled onto the bench after the Champions' League anthem and wondered where Paco was. He'd not seen him all day. His name wasn't on the team sheet. Roy longed to share this moment with his best friend at the club.

If he managed to get onto the pitch.

Halfway thorugh the second half the stadium was quiet. It might as well have been empty for all the noise the so-called fans were making.

Roy could see that most of the children were messing about with their mates. Very few were watching the action. The game was awful, being played at half-pace by players who would never normally get in either first team, all of them more concerned with avoiding injury and collecting their win bonus, than actually putting on a performance. Roy twitched and moved on the bench like he always did. But even *he* was doing it in a lacklustre way.

Roy could hear the shouts of the players quite easily, when they could be bothered to call out. Even Hugo couldn't get the game going.

Tynecaster United led 2-0. But only because the Portuguese team were abysmal – and because the wind was so wild it was breaking up the play. Even so, this was not a memorable night for the ten thousand children coming to see their first ever Champions League game.

Roy caught Ludovico Settembrini watching him twitching and moving for a ball that was a hundred yards away.

'You want to play?' Settembrini asked.

Roy stared at him. 'Er… yes. I mean please. Yes please.'

The Italian coach shrugged.

'Go on, then,' he said with a faint smile. 'Why not? Warm up. You seem more alive than half the players on the pitch. Maybe all of them. Stand up. Get moving. You make your Champions League debut in three minutes.'

Roy had never scored a perfect hat trick before. He'd seen players score them on TV and YouTube. He knew quite well what a perfect hat trick was.

Three goals.

Two shots – one with the left foot and one with the right.

And a header.

But there must always be a first time for everything.

Roy came on with twenty minutes to go. He

was thrilled that his hero, Hugo, jogged over to him from the other wing and ruffled his hair.

'This will be your evening, my friend,' Hugo said. 'I feel it in the air.'

Roy was pleased with Hugo's welcome, because there was no reaction from the crowd. It was awful. Even the children who'd never been to a football match before were disinterested. Roy wanted to change that. He remembered his first live game. The buzz of it. Some of these children might never come back to football.

Roy was determined to change that.

He decided he would play like he used to play for his school, or for Grimroyd, or like last season for Melchester Rovers. Play to enjoy himself, like his mum had said. Just go out and be Roy of the Rovers.

That's what made his mind up.

Scampering up after the ball had gone

over the goal line off a defending player, he arrived on the edge of the area just as the Tynecaster corner came across, ricocheted off a defender's head to Roy.

Roy pounced. With the rocket. A hard hit hammer of a strike from nowhere, the ball screaming into the net, appearing to pass

through the keeper.

3-0.

A good start. And he heard a cheer when some of the children looked up from their games to see the reply on the giant TV screen.

Roy's second touch came when he took a corner. He hit it hard – aiming for the penalty spot – because of the wind rushing through the Tayir Stadium. But the ball didn't reach the penalty spot. It swirled over the first defender and the keeper, then seemed to hang in the air for a few seconds, before it dropped into the net.

Roy had scored from a corner. The roar of the ten thousand children and some adults was weird, a high-pitched celebration. But that was what Roy had wanted, wasn't it? To get the children out of their seats.

Roy punched the air. He'd scored from a corner before. Once. Doing it on purpose.

This goal – however – had been a complete, total fluke.

4-0.

Guy de Flaubert came over to him and patted him on the back. 'This,' the Frenchman smiled, 'I have not seen before. *Très bien.*'

Roy's third touch was even more bizarre. Tynecaster were awarded a penalty. At 4-0 up and Roy the only player on two goals he had a half-thought that his senior teammates might let him, the young debutant, have a go and score a hat trick.

But no. It was clear that was *not* going to happen. His captain – the goalkeeper, Albert Gourmand – snatched the ball up and placed it himself.

'My goal,' he called back to Roy.

Roy watched as Hugo went over to remonstrate with the Frenchman, until Gourmand pushed Hugo on the chest. Hugo frowned, shook his head and shrugged in the direction of Roy.

Roy watched as Gourmand spotted the ball, took three steps back, did a few fast short runs on the spot, then fired the ball at the goal.

Roy – like every good striker should – stood on the edge of the area until Gourmand struck the penalty, then he ran at the goal. He had a half-second to react when the ball, looking like it was heading into the roof of the net, cannoned back at him.

Stooping, he placed his forehead on the speeding ball, which hit the ground in front of him and bounced in off the committed Antunes goalkeeper.

5-0.

A hat trick to Roy.

A perfect hat trick.

Roy felt himself being picked up off the ground. Hugo was there, grinning at

Gourmand who was walking furiously back to his goal.

'Goal for Roy!' Hugo shouted after his French teammate. Then he sighed.

'Sometimes, Roy, I wonder if this is the right club for me and you. This is not a kind place, no?'

WHEN THE WHISTLE for full time went, Roy had touched the ball three times. And scored three goals.

Roy jogged along the length of the main stand where most of the ten thousand children with their free tickets were sitting, cheering his name.

'One Roy Race. There's only one Roy Race,' they cried in a high-pitched chant.

Roy smiled shyly at them and waved.

Ludovico Settembrini strode over to Roy

with the match ball and shook his hand.

'Not bad, Roy Race,' the Tynecaster coach said. 'You've edged yourself up a little.' He handed Roy the ball, with its Champions League stars and logo stamped on two sides.

'But before that...' Settembrini added.

'Yes, Coach?'

'I need you to keep these adoring children with the club. Later in the week we are having a fun day for fans. I want you to train some children for me.'

'Me?'

'Yes, you?'

'But I don't know anything about kids,' Roy said, wondering how he was going to get out of that one. It was weird, the idea of playing in the Champions League had made him nervous, but not as nervous as teaching a bunch of kids how to play the game made him feel.

17

THURSDAY AFTERNOON. A day off after his Champions League debut and hat trick. Roy and his dad were in the front room, Dad in his wheelchair, Roy, legs dangled over the side of an armchair as he played FIFA.

In reaction to his hat trick, Dad had patted his son on the back, half-smiling. But no words.

His mum had hugged him, saying nothing either.

Rocky was the only one who reacted to Roy's Champions League debut with words.

'I can't believe you helped them win a

game 5-0,' Rocky spat. 'Can't you remember how that used to make you feel? When Tynecaster hammered someone you used to be as gutted as you were if Rovers lost. Now you'd doing it for them. I can't speak to you.'

'Cheers,' Roy said, remembering exactly the feelings she was referring to and wondering if he was doing the right thing. A hat trick in the Champions League was every player's dream. But was it a dream if it was for them?

But Rocky had gone now. It was just Dad and Roy. That – for today – was just how Roy wanted it.

Both of them were wearing their Melchester Rovers tops. The electric heater in the fireplace was on. It was autumn now, sheets of rain thrashing against the small bay window in the front of their terraced house.

FIFA was one of the things Roy and his

dad did together, taking Melchester Rovers to the heights of European glory. And beyond. Today they were guiding Rovers through the Champions League knock-out stages. The irony was not lost on Roy. Or his dad.

Because of his brain tumour, Dad was unable to connect his brain to his voice box most of the time. That meant he could make noises, gesture yes or no with his head and with his good hand. But it was only once or twice a week that Dad managed to force a word out.

Roy lived for these words. They were like signposts on a desolate and misty moor for him.

Today, more than ever, Roy wanted a word from his dad. Or two. He was going to ask him if breaking into Cleaver's house was the right thing to do. If his dad could just say *Do it* then Roy would do it.

On FIFA it was an away tie against Surreal Salvador, the Spanish Champions. But Roy was way off his game. There was a reason: on his way home from training at Tynecaster, he had experienced a couple of things that unsettled him.

The first was when he was jogging back home along the canal through the city centre, hoodie up, so no-one would recognise him. As he ran he had been thinking about whether he really should break into Barry Cleaver's house at all. Ducking to go low under a canal tunnel, and bursting out of the other side, he nearly knocked a pair of nuns coming the other way into the water. After apologising he ran up from the canal, through the bus station and up the terrible two hundred, a killer flight of stone steps that he liked to push himself up, to force his fitness.

As he ran hard up the steps, Roy heard a

rattling sound, like a train or a heavy lorry. But the sound was above him. He looked up, slowing as he reached the top of the hill.

Above him there was a police helicopter, circling as if they were looking for someone, or following them. Roy frowned. He'd watched a film once with his dad about a

man who had committed a crime and was paranoid that a helicopter was following him. Roy was pretty sure helicopters were not following him and that God had not sent nuns to block his way. But it worried him. Were these strange events signs?

Roy tried his hardest to get Melchester past the Surreal Salvador FC defence, but

it was like they'd been programmed not to concede a goal by FIFA. All Roy's usual routes to goal just didn't work and the game had simply decided Roy must lose.

All the time he played, Roy was thinking what his dad might say.

Dad... I'm going to break into Barry Cleaver's house and steal a box of files that will prove he is corrupt and save Rovers from destruction.

What would his dad say to that?

Roy was used to second-guessing his father's replies. It was something he did now when he had a big decision to make.

Great idea, Roy, his dad might say. *Saving the club is more important than breaking some silly law.* Maybe. Or maybe not. Maybe he'd say: *It's wrong to break into someone's house. Full stop. End of.*

Roy fumbled with his controller as his

players failed to break down the Spanish FIFA side. He was well aware that he was frowning and that his dad would be able to work out there was something wrong, something more than FIFA going into a weird setting where, whatever you did, you couldn't score.

'What?' Dad said.

Roy looked at his dad, his frown falling away. A word from his dad always gave him such a rush of adrenaline. But he had to handle this carefully. Very carefully.

'I need to ask you something,' he said.

Dad nodded and looked Roy in the eye. But, then that cold feeling was running through Roy. The one that was his body warning him. Should he say anything? Should he make his dad worry about him? He knew – deep down – that his dad would disapprove. Knew he'd say no to committing a crime.

Dad was still looking at him. Now he lifted his right hand and placed it on Roy's arm. Since his dad had lost the ability to speak and move, his eyes had taken on new powers. You could tell exactly what he wanted. Now Roy had to say something.

'I've been asked to do something I don't want to do,' Roy said.

Dad raised his right eyebrow.

Roy swallowed, then knew what he had to say. Not the break-in. It felt wrong to talk to his dad about that. He'd ask about something else.

'The coach at Tynecaster wants me to do a day of training children to play football. Like a community event. But I don't want to. I think I should train harder all the time, so I can get a place in the team. I'm not going to take part.'

Dad shook his head, then closed his eyes. When he opened his eyes, Dad said 'Do it.'

ROY WAS THRILLED to be told what to do by his dad. He missed that.

He was surprised how nervous he felt when he arrived at Tynecaster United's training ground, on the edge of the huge forest to the north of Melchester. Its high wire fences. Its perfect pitches. The rumour was that – before building the facility – Tynecaster had had twenty thousand trees felled to make space for the pitches and buildings.

A cluster of newspaper reporters and cameramen called his name.

'ROY! What was it like to score a

Champions League hat trick?'

'Aren't you glad you moved up a few leagues now, Roy?'

Roy put his head down and walked through the throng of reporters. He hated this. It made him nervous too. That he might say something back, make another media mistake.

Then a man was in front of him, holding

something white to his chest.

Roy stepped back as a cameraman moved in and took shot after shot of him.

Roy saw what he was holding against him. An England shirt. With a number nine and his name – ROY RACE – on the back.

'Next stop Wembley?' the man shouted.

Roy walked on. Said nothing. Didn't look into the camera. And was glad to see a group of twelve children waiting for him with Settembrini.

Roy's coach introduced the mixture of boys and girls, all aged around eight, to Roy.

'Welcome to our open day, children. This is Roy Race. He is a local lad who is in our development squad. Has anyone heard of him?'

All the children's hands went up with a cheer. Some of them seemed to be bouncing up and down with excitement, dressed in their Tynecaster tops. Roy understood that his hat trick had made an impact. He imagined it helped that ten thousand local children had been given free tickets for the game. It was likely most of them had seen his three goals live or on TV.

But one boy was not cheering and jumping up and down. He had blond hair and a kind face. And... he was wearing a Melchester Rovers top. At Tynecaster!

Roy smiled at the boy. That's just the sort of thing he would have done himself as a kid: go to a big thing at Tynecaster and brazenly wear his Melchester Rovers' shirt. The boy didn't smile back. He had his arms folded and he looked cross.

'This is my son, Hunter,' the boy's dad said, coming forward to shake Roy's hand. 'He's still a bit unhappy about... you know.'

Roy nodded and frowned back at Hunter.

He was desperate to explain to the boy why he'd left Melchester Rovers and how – every morning he woke up and remembered that he was no longer a Rovers' player – that it felt like a stake had been driven through his heart. But he couldn't. Roy knew he had to move on, make out he was a happy, carefree footballer, whose job was to inspire these children.

He had to grow up, be an adult, be the professional footballer he now was.

Roy quickly got the children running round a set of cones to warm up. He told them why: they had to loosen their muscles, so to avoid injury. Then he had them passing balls to each other fast, making them stand closer and closer to each other.

'Two touches,' he told them, getting into his role. 'Control it, then pass. Faster and faster.'

The children were laughing as they played.

The mums and dads who had come with them smiled. Roy knew this was going okay.

'Shall we take some shots, now?' Roy asked.

The children agreed.

'Who wants to go in goal?'

Hunter pointed at Roy. Roy rolled his eyes. He hated going in goal. The last time he'd done it his sister had made a right fool of him. But Roy was also desperate to make Hunter happy. So he did as he was told.

For the next few minutes Roy faced all of the children, letting them all score at least one of their three shots. Only one – Hunter – scored all three of his. And Roy was trying to save them too!

At the end of the session most of the parents thanked Roy. One mum squeezed his shoulder, keeping her hand on his arm, and told him he was a natural. Then Hunter and his dad waited to be last. Roy knew the boy had something to say. He hoped it would be nice.

'Hi, Hunter,' Roy said, squatting to be level with him. 'I like your shirt.'

The boy frowned. 'Do you?' he asked, his voice challenging.

Roy blinked and looked at the boy. Had he heard him right?

'What's that?'

'*Do* you like my shirt?' Hunter said, his voice softening as he felt his dad squat behind him. 'You used to have one, but you don't like it anymore.'

'Erm...' Roy said.

'Hunter,' the boy's dad said. 'Be nice. We talked about this. Say your piece, but be respectful.'

The boy coughed, then started. 'You were my hero. I wanted to be a footballer like you.

You wore the football top I've always loved, that my dad loves. And me and my dad have always been Melchester supporters. And I really thought, with you up front we'd get back to being a great team again. But... you just went for the money. Didn't you?'

Roy tried to speak, but it was hard to get

the words out.

'Didn't you?'

Roy nodded. 'It was all about the money.'

Hunter's dad intervened: 'But we've talked about it, Hunter. Roy wants the money to help his mum and dad, not because he is greedy and wants it for himself. I think we can both see that Roy is upset he can't wear that shirt.'

Roy nearly laughed. It was true. There was nothing he would like more than to rip the Tynecaster shirt off, throw it to the ground and walk out of the training ground. That was his dream.

'I still wear Melchester tops at home,' Roy smiled. 'With my dad. We both have tops and we play as Rovers on FIFA. I've even got Mel Rovers pyjamas.'

Hunter tried to smile.

'Sorry, Roy,' Hunter's dad said. 'I'll

explain it to him.'

Roy watched as the boy and his dad walked away.

When they had gone, Roy knew he had to do something. This was all wrong. He saw himself in Hunter. He would have said the same thing when he was that age. Would have felt the same thing too.

But what could he do to make Hunter feel better? Hunter and all the other Hunters across Melchester?

There had to be something.

Roy was wearing his black hoodie and black jeans again. And his Converse trainers, dark blue. He waited until Mum and Dad had gone to bed – Dad used the chairlift like a natural now – and then Roy crept out of the back door to jog to the park next to Barry Cleaver's house.

He and Ffion were going in.

Tonight.

The Race family had a nice evening, all four together, laughing and playing cards in front of the fire. Roy hadn't seen Mum this happy for two years. He was so relieved he had not told either of them about the break-in. Rocky had been smiling conspiratorially at him all evening. Roy had wrongly assumed that she was just pleased that they were having a happy family time with no arguments.

He was wrong.

Roy closed the back door quietly. Outside

now, the night was quiet, except for a familiar fluttering of wings somewhere in the trees.

Roy breathed out.

He was clear.

'STOP!' A loud voice shocked him. He threw himself against the side wall of the house, feeing like his heart had stopped.

Then he saw her. Standing there. Laughing.

'Bit jumpy, aren't you?' his sister chuckled.

'I'm not.' Roy knew he sounded defensive.

'And there was me thinking you were about to break into Barry Cleaver's house and steal some evidence,' Rocky said.

Roy swallowed. 'Why would you think that?' he asked.

'Deduction,' Rocky said.

Roy didn't know what she meant. He just stared at her.

'It means I'm cleverer than you,' she clarified.

'I'm not,' Roy said. 'Not breaking in anywhere, I mean. I'm just going to meet Ffion. Go for a drive. You know...'

Rocky grinned. 'You've never been able to lie,' she laughed. 'You're a boring footballer. You'll have it written down somewhere that you need to be in bed by 10 p.m. with only a glass of water drunk since 7 p.m. so you

sleep well. And that you only see your love interest on your free weekend evening and one afternoon a week.'

Roy shrugged. His sister was a monster. Like some maniac from one of those psychologically worrying films.

'Tell me… Don't tell me…' she said. 'But I want you to know that I'd be proud of you if that *was* your plan. It might be wrong to break into someone's house. But sometimes there's more to a crime than first meets the eye: sometimes you have to do something bad to be able to do what's good.'

Rocky gave her brother a kiss on the cheek, then turned and disappeared into the house.

Roy could feel himself frowning. He was torn now. Torn to shreds. As he stood, stunned, he heard the noise of wings flapping again and looked up.

The owl. The white owl. For the second time in a week. What was that about? Was it an omen? Like the nuns and the police helicopter?

Worrying that he was losing his mind, Roy stepped out of the shadows and brushed the brick dust from the side of the house off his hoodie.

Whatever!

Nothing was going to change his mind now. He knew what he was going to do. And, with that, Roy Race jogged down the hill to meet Ffion.

The events of the next two or three hours could well be life changing.

THEY MET ON the far side of Hinchliffe Park, where Ffion had parked her car. Neither of them spoke. They exchanged a quick kiss and began walking through the park hand in hand, like a normal girlfriend and boyfriend out for a walk. They mustn't draw attention to themselves.

Roy was desperate to say they shouldn't do this, that it was wrong. But they had promised each other they wouldn't speak as they carried out their task: they'd be less likely to be caught. So silence reigned.

Through the park, in the shadows of

the trees and along the wide, leafy street where Barry Cleaver lived. Roy felt his hand sweating. Or was it Ffion's? Maybe it was both of them. Perhaps they were both nervous. What were they doing?

This was Roy's state of mind: question after question, warning light after warning light, omen after omen.

They made it to the far end of the street to an ostentatious black wrought iron gate, with 'The Meat' in golden lettering across it.

'I think we're here,' Roy laughed. But it was no genuine laugh: he could feel his breathing shallowing, giving away his nervousness. He glanced at Ffion: she looked pink-faced, stressed. They stopped. Ffion nodded at Roy. That was the sign for them to begin, to find a way to climb into Barry Cleaver's garden.

Ffion pointed at the tree.

Roy nodded. He understood.

Then Ffion made as if she was about to climb it. But Roy put his hand on her shoulder. She looked round. Roy pointed at himself. Ffion shrugged. Then Roy began to climb the tree. Even though his legs were trembling and his hands still sweating, he made it above the level of the wall. And there – on a small turning circle – was Barry Cleaver's car.

On the back seat was a box.

The box.

This was perfect. Easy. This was like a gift. Almost too easy. Because now they didn't need to break into the Melchester Rovers' owner's house. Just his car. Roy just had to get over the wall.

Then Dad's voice came into his head, clear and strong.

It's wrong and you know it's wrong, Roy. You mustn't do it.

Roy breathed in, then sighed.

After hesitating, he dropped down from the tree and faced Ffion. She brushed some dirt off his trouser leg.

'The box is in his car,' he whispered close to her ear. 'On the drive. I can actually see it.'

Ffion stuck her thumb up, moving towards the fence.

'But I can't do it.' Roy told her, dreading Ffion's reaction to what he had to say to her. 'It's wrong.'

He was not expecting Ffion to throw her arms around him, but she did. She squeezed him hard.

'It is wrong,' Ffion agreed. 'Of course it is.' Silence.

The tree Roy had climbed seemed to shiver as a gust of wind took some of its leaves off. The clouds were moving rapidly across the sky and suddenly they were caught in a beam of moonlight.

'Meaning...' Roy started.

'... we can't help Mel Rovers,' Ffion replied. 'And you stay at that... other football team?' Ffion sounded miserable. Resigned.

Roy half-thought that maybe they *should*

go ahead with the break-in. Just to make Ffion happy. Would he do that? he wondered. Commit a crime to stop Ffion feeling sad?

Ffion hugged him again.

'It's the right thing to not go through with it,' she told him. 'Don't doubt yourself.'

'I know,' Roy's voice caught in his throat.

Roy and Ffion turned and walked across the park, leaving Barry Cleaver's house – and any hope of them saving Melchester Rovers – behind.

ROCKY WAS WAITING when Roy arrived home, a half-drunk glass of apple juice in front of her on the wooden tabletop. The kitchen looked small under the bright strip light on the ceiling.

'You look dashing,' Rocky said, lifting her head from the kitchen table. 'Sorry... I mean... shocking.'

Roy shrugged. He probably did look shocking. He was shattered. It was after one in the morning. He looked at his reflection in the window, blacked out by the night. He saw lines on his face. He looked more like his dad than himself tonight.

'Bed,' he frowned, walking past his sister.

But Rocky had him by the arm. 'Hang on,' she said. 'Did you get the box from Cleaver's?'

Roy considered lying. But they both knew that he was rubbish at lying and didn't really want to either. His sister could read him like a matchday programme, anyway.

'No,' he told her, his voice cracking. 'We saw it. In his car on the driveway. But we decided not to do it. Breaking and entering. Theft. You know? It's wrong.'

'You idiot...' Rocky stopped herself.

'What?' Roy snatched his arm away. 'Why am I an idiot?'

Rocky opened her mouth to speak, then, looking at the back door, said: 'Oh... nothing. You go up. I'll just finish my drink.'

Roy went to bed quietly, not even turning his light on. He lay in the dark thinking about what would have happened if he had gone over the wall and had stolen the box file.

Could he have saved Melchester Rovers?

He had had his chance. But not taken it.

Dropping off to sleep ten minutes later, Roy heard a click, then footsteps. He lay there trying to work out who it could have been in nearby houses, leaving home at half-one at night. He thought about asking Rocky if she'd heard the noise, just in case there was something going on outside. But he remembered: Rocky had not come upstairs yet...

Rocky...

Not upstairs...

Footsteps outside...

Roy jumped to his feet and scrambled to put his clothes on. Finding his sister was not, as he had expected, in her bedroom, he raced down the stairs.

Rocky had gone to Cleaver's house. Her glass was still on the table. She was mad. And Roy had to stop her. If there was time.

As HE RAN across town, Roy imagined what would happen to Rocky if she was caught. Would she have to go to a children's prison? How would she cope with that? How would *Mum* and *Dad* cope with that? It would be too much. There were so many pressures on his parents. Rocky going to prison would finish them off.

It took Roy twelve minutes to run down into town, across Hinchliffe Park and to Cleaver's house, surrounded by its wall. As he came round the corner, Cleaver's house before him, he saw his sister disappearing into the football chairman's garden, dropping down from the wall.

Roy understood that his sister was seconds away from breaking the law. He had to do something. But the big question was – now that she was knee deep in this – should he stop her or help her?

WHEN HE HAD scrambled to the top of the wall, lifted himself to the top, Roy looked down into Barry Cleaver's front garden and drive.

There – staring back at him – was Rocky with a half-smile on her face. The other half of her expression was of panic. She had the box file in her hands.

'How do I get out?' she moaned.

There was no way out. The overhanging tree had allowed her to climb in, but it was no use helping her get out.

Roy frowned. Now what? Help his sister commit a crime? Or leave her? He had no choice. He had to do the right thing.

Roy put his hand down. 'I'll lift you up,' he said.

Rocky handed Roy the box file. He didn't need to think about what he should do. He had one job: get his sister out of there. Just as he dragged his sister over the wall, an alarm

sounded. A mournful high-pitched wailing that set off a dog in a nearby house. Lights came on. And Roy knew that trouble would be here. And soon.

They jumped off the wall together, Roy keeping his balance as he hit the floor, the box file still jammed under his arm.

Then they ran.

'Fast up the street,' Roy gasped. 'Then we can slow down in the park.'

Rocky said nothing as she edged ahead of Roy.

Even though she was probably terrified, Rocky making this a race made Roy smile. Just like earlier in the week, she wanted to beat him, however dangerous their predicament was.

They ran hard. Then harder. Over the main road and into the woods. Both of them laughing.

Rocky stopped and waited for her brother among the trees.

'I win again,' she said.

'Hmmm,' Roy said, a sudden flash of anger overwhelming him. 'You idiot. You just stole something.'

Rocky stood up, hands on hips, sweat pouring off her face.

'The car was unlocked,' she said. 'And anyway, it was justified.'

'Yeah?'

'Yeah. The Meat Cleaver stole the club. He is chopping it to pieces like one of his cow carcasses. The police can't touch him, even though he has broken a hundred laws, we know. He burned Mel Park down, Roy. I just tried to even the score. A bit. So don't…' a wobble of emotion in Rocky's voice made her hesitate, 'you call me an idiot. Or you're the idiot.'

*　*　*

THEY WAITED FOR the sirens to quieten down, before emerging from Hinchliffe Park.

There was only one car parked on the back road that went into town from the park. Roy and Rocky passed it without noticing the silhouette of someone sat in the driver's seat.

Once past the car, Roy heard a car door open.

'Keep walking,' he said to his sister. 'Don't look round.'

Rocky looked round just as the car's headlights came on, bathing them in blinding yellow light.

'I said…' Roy started.

'It's Ffion,' Rocky interrupted him.

'What?' Roy turned round.

Ffion was clapping her hands. 'I don't

know how you did it,' she smiled. 'But you did. I came back. I was going to… but… that doesn't matter now. Can I give you a lift to the newspaper offices?'

THERE WAS A woman on the desk behind a rotating door at the newspaper head offices. She looked like a security guard, and she eyed Ffion nervously through the glass. Ffion stood there, hood up, the box file in her hands in front of her, then gestured her to come.

The security guard approached, looking wary. There was someone at her door, with a hood up, at two in the morning.

Not a normal situation.

Roy sat in the car with Rocky watching. Ffion had insisted she deliver the box. If there was any come back, any CCTV, she could say she found the box. There was nothing to link the theft from Barry Cleaver's property with her.

'This is for Becky Goff,' Ffion shouted.

Listening from the car, Roy felt a rush of pride. That was a good call.

The woman pointed to the floor. 'Leave it there,' she said. 'Open it.'

Ffion nodded, put the box file on the ground and opened it to show the papers inside.

'She needs it for her story,' Ffion shouted.

The security guard opened the door and gathered the box, closing it.

'Shall I say who left it for her?' the guard asked.

Ffion shook her head.

'Just say it's from Militant Melchester. Please?'

The woman nodded. Then locked the

door. Ffion noticed that she was wearing a Melchester Rovers badge on her lapel.

THE MORNING AFTER the night before and Roy was playing his second game starting for the Tynecaster United Under-18s. versus Walford at the Tynecaster training ground, in the shadow of the Tayir Stadium.

After the dramatic events of the last few days, Roy was pleased to be playing football. Roy had decided to take his mum's advice. Once he was over the white line and on the football pitch, nothing mattered but the game.

That was it.

Football.

Football. Full. Stop.

Midway through the first half, Roy took a pass from Paco Diaz, his back to the last defender. Holding off the defender, he looked up and heard Hugo calling from the touchline.

'Turn him,' the Brazilian shouted. 'Turn him.'

Trusting Hugo, Roy rolled the ball forward with his left foot, then touched it with his heel, nudging it between the legs of his marker. Then – in one movement, dropping his shoulder – Roy turned and went after the ball.

He'd skinned the Walford defender and felt the confused player's arm come out to pull him back, but Roy had all his weight ahead of him now and shrugged off the attempted foul.

One-on-one with the keeper now.

But the keeper – like Roy – had chosen to go for the ball and was closing in fast, giving Roy one second to decide what to do.

He didn't think.

He just drew his foot back and hit the bottom of the ball, lifting it over the keeper, whose arms clamoured at the air before he fell on his penalty spot, the ball thrashing into the back of the net behind him.

Roy looked over to Hugo, who stuck his thumbs up.

Football.

Football. Full. Stop.

Nothing else mattered.

On the pitch he was Roy Race, footballer. He was in the groove. Nothing could stop him now. Except it could. And it was about to.

At half time, Roy smiled and began to walk to the side of the pitch to listen to Hugo's half time talk. He was surprised to see Hugo, then, walking towards him, onto the pitch, away from some of the other Tynecaster players.

Not normal behaviour.

Roy looked deep into Hugo's eyes and saw something. Something to worry about. Now, as they came face to face, Roy heard mobile phones going off, saw people staring, then pointing.

At him.

'What's going on?' Roy asked.

'You… there's been… oh, my friend, I do not know how to tell you.'

'Dad?' Roy moaned. 'Is it Dad?'

That was always his first thought. Dad. Was Dad okay?

Hugo's hand was on Roy's shoulder now. 'No. Not so bad,' the Brazilian international calmed him. 'Your dad is good. But you, my friend, are no longer a Tynecaster United player.'

'What?' Roy didn't get it.

'You play for Melchester Rovers now,' Hugo told him.

Roy felt a smile creeping across his face, a rush of excitement up his spine.

Hugo explained. Barry Cleaver been met at the airport on the way back from Portugal and had quickly cracked under pressure in the police station.

He'd admitted Roy and Paco's contracts were phoney.

Tynecaster had heard about it.

Now they wanted Roy and Paco out.

'They're sending security to remove you from the premises,' Hugo said. 'Come with me. I'll get you out.'

'Thanks, Hugo,' Roy said, his head spinning, but a smile playing on his lips.

'Paco,' Hugo shouted. 'This way!'

Paco jogged over to them.

Hugo quickly led Roy and Paco towards the car park. But it was too late. Two security guards were jogging towards him, one of them speaking into a radio.

Behind them a camera crew was lining up a shot.

The first security guard grabbed Roy, yanking his arm.

'Out, you,' he said.

Roy pulled his arm away and pushed the guard. 'Get off me,' he shouted, as Hugo stood between him and the guards.

'You'd better go, my friends. I will meet you soon. When it is nicer.'

'Thanks mate,' Roy said, heading for the gates.

Seeing a second camera crew and a trio of photographers focussed on him – and angry that he'd been hustled out of the training ground – Roy, in one swift movement, tore off his Tynecaster United shirt, and, without looking back, tossed it behind him, then wiped his hands on his shorts.

Tynecaster United was over.

Roy looked into the eyes of his friend, Paco Diaz.

'To Mel Park, then,' Roy laughed.

Roy Race and Paco Diaz walked from the far side of the car park, where they agreed to meet before this most important day of days.

Only a few days ago they had been playing football for the Champions of Europe, among some of the world's greatest footballers ever, men who had won World Cups, Ballon D'Ors and travelled the world in private jets and helicopters.

Today, they'd got the bus from town to Mel Park, a 1950s stadium, half of which had been consumed by fire. Seeing the great hole in the stand where the fire had ripped a hole in his football club, Roy stopped and stared at Mel Park and felt that shiver of excitement run up his spine. The shiver of excitement he had missed so much while playing at Tynecaster. Because, despite his fears and sadness about the state of Mel Park and Melchester Rovers, how his club seemed to be on the edge of a catastrophe, he was happy.

He was home.

Back.

Back at the place he most loved in the world. More than his home. More than the Moor. But what was he coming back to?

Melchester Rovers was on its knees.

The stadium half-burned down.

But it wasn't all bad news. Since a certain box of papers had been handed over to the *Melchester Leader*, things had changed.

For the better.

'Right then…' Roy said, turning to Paco Diaz and giving words to his thoughts. 'First day back…'

'To what, exactly?' Paco asked.

Now they were closer, Roy could see a large crane above the stadium, moving in a slow circle, a chain swaying as it did. There were JCBs and trucks too, clearing the rubble, ripping the stadium down.

And nothing was being rebuilt.

'Roy Race, my friend, Paco is not superstitious or one to look for signs…'

Roy frowned. He did not want to hear what his friend said to him.

'But?' he said reluctantly.

'But,' Paco sighed. 'Melchester Rovers look dead and buried to me.'

Roy said nothing. Paco was right. What could he say?

'I mean…' Paco went on. 'Three days ago

we were training at the Tayir Stadium, space-age, always the singing, always the dancing, as you often say.'

'All singing, all dancing,' Roy corrected Paco quietly.

Paco let out a long, pained groan. 'We were with the Premier League Champions,' he said. 'At Tynecaster. And now...'

As they walked on, hoodies up, so that nobody had recognised them yet, Roy noticed a cluster of people standing near the front of the main stand. One holding a camera, one asking questions and another.

Roy squinted to see who was being interviewed on camera. She was wearing a jacket and pencil skirt, dark blue. Her hair was tied up above her head. She was carrying a small notebook and pen.

Becky Goff.

Rocky grabbed Paco and went to stand

near the journalist to listen to what she had to say.

The journalist had been busy. She'd used the papers Rocky had left for her and written a story that had changed everything.

'A source of mine,' Goff boasted, 'that I had been working with, directing in fact, for months of investigative journalism... delivered to my offices in a midnight run... all the evidence I needed to save Melchester Rovers.'

The journalist paused, aware that everyone around her was listening.

'The evidence showed that Barry Cleaver has been bleeding this football club dry for years. That the transfers of Rovers' two greatest talents for a generation – Paco Diaz and Roy Race – were illegal. Cleaver and the football agent, Alan Talbot, have broken dozens of laws, and were both arrested on their return from a golfing holiday in

Portugal together earlier this week.'

A massive cheer, then a question from the crowd. Coming from a man holding a small Yorkshire Terrier.

'And the thirty points? Diaz? And Race?'

Roy smiled from behind his hoodie. He'd missed the likes of Fred. Fred represented everything that was good about football. He was a proper fan. Of a proper club.

'I understand that the football authorities,' Becky Goff went on, 'are removing the thirty points deduction.'

A cheer meant the journalist had to stop speaking. When it had calmed down, she had something else to say.

'And,' she went on, 'I am thrilled to tell all Melchester Rovers fans that your prodigal sons – Roy Race and Paco Diaz – are coming back from their nightmare transfer to Tynecaster United.'

Another cheer.

Both players' names were chanted.

Roy and Paco looked into each others' eyes and smiled. This was good. This was very good.

Then, with a flourish, Becky Goff turned to face Roy and Paco, her interview over, her iPhone out. There was no doubt she had her microphone on.

'And here they are,' she said, seamlessly switching from interviewee to interviewer. 'Morning Roy, Paco,' she said.

Roy froze. The smile drained from his face. All eyes were on him. Most notably those of the journalist, Becky Goff.

Did she know about his involvement with the box of papers?

'BECKY GOFF, MELCHESTER *Leader*,' the jounalist said. 'Can you tell us what you know about the dramatic events of the last few days?'

'We know who you are, Becky,' Roy replied.

'I know, Roy, but we're on the record now, eh?'

Roy winced.

That was the first thing that Johnny Dexter had taught him, when he'd first started making a name for himself at Melchester Rovers, one night as he gave him a lift home in the club minibus.

Be careful what you say. Especially to a journalist.

But if you had been involved in a burglary that threatened your future, your sister's future, your mum and dad's health and your football club's future, you had to be even

more cautious.

Becky Goff filled the silence.

'I wanted to know how you both feel,' she asked. 'About your club.'

Roy swallowed. Now what? The eyes of the fans around him were on him. The TV camera was pointing at him. A microphone was stuck under his nose.

He had to say something. Didn't he?

Then, suddenly, Becky Goff flinched and Roy heard a terrible cracking, then crash after crash after crash, as clouds of dust and ash poured from the main stand.

A huge piece of roof was sliding slowly away from them onto the pitch, taking the stand with it. The roar was appalling. Everyone had their hands over their ears as a cloud of dust consumed them all.

When everything had settled down, light streaming in from where there used to be a huge edifice of corrugated iron and wood, Roy looked through his fingers and stared in horror.

Mel Park was finished. A second stand had come down.

Devastated.

And Becky Goff was talking into the camera.

'Now the whole stadium seems to have collapsed,' she said, barely concealing her grin. 'Melchester Rovers might have their thirty points back, but without an owner and without a stadium, can they continue? Look at this carnage. I mean... does anyone see a future for this football club?'

Silence met Becky Goff's question.

The hundreds of fans were stunned. Nobody had an answer.

Then a voice.

A child's voice.

A boy stepped forward. He was wearing a Melchester Rovers' top.

Roy recognised the boy. It was Hunter. The boy he'd met at Tynecaster. The boy who had been so disappointed in him.

'I see a future,' Hunter said. 'I see Roy Race. He's the greatest footballer in this country. He never wanted to leave Melchester Rovers. He did it for his mum and his dad. He told me. And, now that he's back, this club is going to be okay. He's our future.'

Thank You

As ALWAYS I had a lot of help with this book. Roy needs the likes of Hugo, Johnny Dexter, Ffion, Settembrini, his dad, his mum... even Rocky, to make his football as good as it can be.

My support team with *From the Ashes* were Team Roy, including editor, Rob Power, and illustrators Lisa Henke and Dan Cornwell.

Huge thanks to Simon Robinson, who is my Roy of the Rovers expert and consultant.

Thanks, too, to the children and staff of Rosehill School in Kent, to whom this book is dedicated. Notably head of sports, Simon Hinchliffe, for all his help.

Finally, thanks to John and Hunter Still for helping make the end of the book work better – and for agreeing to be the characters to make that happen.

THE STORY CONTINUES!

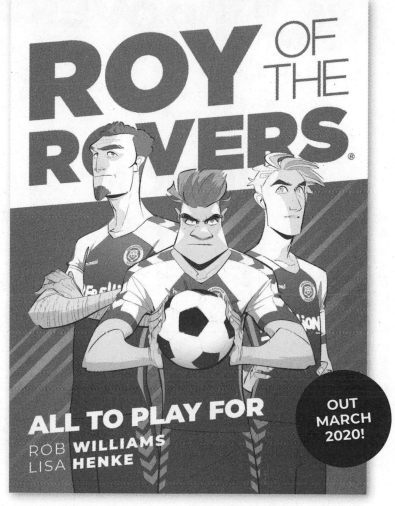

ROY OF THE **ROVERS**®

ALL TO PLAY FOR

ROB **WILLIAMS**
LISA **HENKE**

OUT MARCH 2020!

Roy returns to Rovers – but can Racey, back at Melchester after his stint with Tynecaster, pull the club back from the bring of relegation? He's got a huge task ahead of him in **ALL TO PLAY FOR**, the latest all-new *Roy of the Rovers* graphic novel!

For more **ROY OF THE ROVERS** find us online:

www.royoftherovers.com

ROY OF THE ROVERS

THE FIRST SEASON

Keep track of every new **Roy of the Rovers** book here!
Don't forget to tick the boxes as you read each one.

FICTION

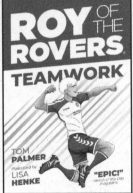

BOOK 1
SCOUTED

Author: Tom Palmer
Out: October 2018
ISBN: 978-1-78108-698-8

Roy Race is the most
talented striker in
Melchester – but is he
good enough to catch
the eye of the Melchester
Rovers scouts?

READ? ☐

BOOK 2
TEAMWORK

Author: Tom Palmer
Out: February 2019
ISBN: 978-1-78108-707-7

Life gets tricky for Roy as
he adjusts to life in the
spotlight. Fortune and
glory await, but can Roy
juggle football, fame and
family?

READ? ☐

BOOK 3
PLAY-OFFS

Author: Tom Palmer
Out: May 2019
ISBN: 978-1-78108-722-0

Crunch time for Rovers: the
end of the season is here,
the club is in deep trouble,
and it's down to Roy to
bring a bit of hope back to
the Melchester faithful.

READ? ☐

COMICS

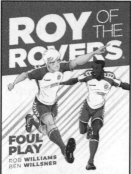

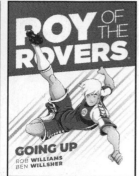

BOOK 1
KICK-OFF

Writer: Rob Williams
Artist: Ben Willsher
Out: November 2018
ISBN: 978-1-78108-652-0

Roy Race is 16, talented, and desperate to make it as a footballer. But is he good enough for Melchester Rovers? Now's the time to prove if he's got what it takes to become Roy of the Rovers.

READ? ☐

BOOK 2
FOUL PLAY

Writer: Rob Williams
Artist: Ben Willsher
Out: March 2019
ISBN: 978-1-78108-669-8

Roy picks up an injury that puts him on the sidelines, and suddenly there's competition for his place as a brand new - and brilliant - striker is brought in by the management...

READ? ☐

BOOK 3
GOING UP

Writer: Rob Williams
Artist: Ben Willsher
Out: June 2019
ISBN: 978-1-78108-673-5

Roy and the team have battled through a tough season, but have they got enough left to get promoted? Or will they fall at the final hurdle and see the club sold by its greedy owner?

READ? ☐

ROY OF THE ROVERS GOES DIGITAL!

Roy of the Rovers is back, with brand new comics and books starring Roy Race and the mighty Melchester Rovers – and now you can keep up to date with all things Roy on your smartphone or tablet!

Through the new *Roy of the Rovers* app, you'll be able to read the awesome new stories, grab some free comics, and even play Rovers-themed word games!

SEARCH FOR *ROY OF THE ROVERS* IN YOUR APP STORE OF CHOICE!

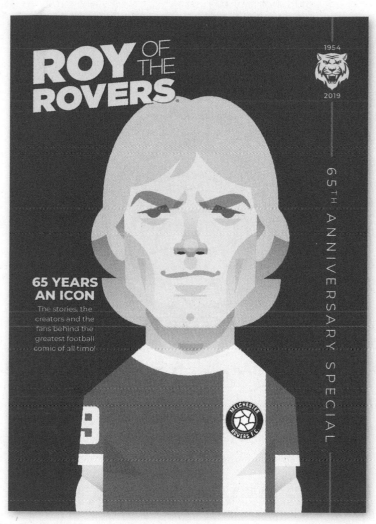

Celebrate the greatest football comic of all time with the **65TH ANNIVERSARY SPECIAL**! Join us as we take a stroll through six unforgettable decades and chart the stories, the creators, the goals and the glory that made *Roy of the Rovers* the phenomenon it is today!

For more **ROY OF THE ROVERS** find us online:

www.royoftherovers.com

YOUR REVIEWS MATTER!

Enjoy this book? Got something to say?
Leave a review on Amazon, GoodReads or with your
favourite bookseller and let the world know!